WS

Picture a Poem

Gina Douthwaite

RED FOX

PICTURE A POEM

A RED FOX BOOK 0 09 932071 1

First published in Great Britain by Hutchinson,
an imprint of Random House Children's Books

Hutchinson edition published 1994
This Red Fox edition published 2002

1 3 5 7 9 10 8 6 4 2

Red Fox Books are published by Random House Children's Books,
61–63 Uxbridge Road, London W5 5SA,
a division of The Random House Group Ltd,
in Australia by Random House Australia (Pty) Ltd,
20 Alfred Street, Milsons Point, Sydney, NSW 2061, Australia,
in New Zealand by Random House New Zealand Ltd,
18 Poland Road, Glenfield, Auckland 10, New Zealand,
and in South Africa by Random House (Pty) Ltd,
Endulini, 5A Jubilee Road, Parktown 2193, South Africa

THE RANDOM HOUSE GROUP Limited Reg. No. 954009
www.kidsatrandomhouse.co.uk

A CIP catalogue record for this book is available from the British Library.

Printed in Hong Kong by Midas Printing Limited

For Louise and Katy — the 'Sisters'

CONTENTS

FUN and GAMES

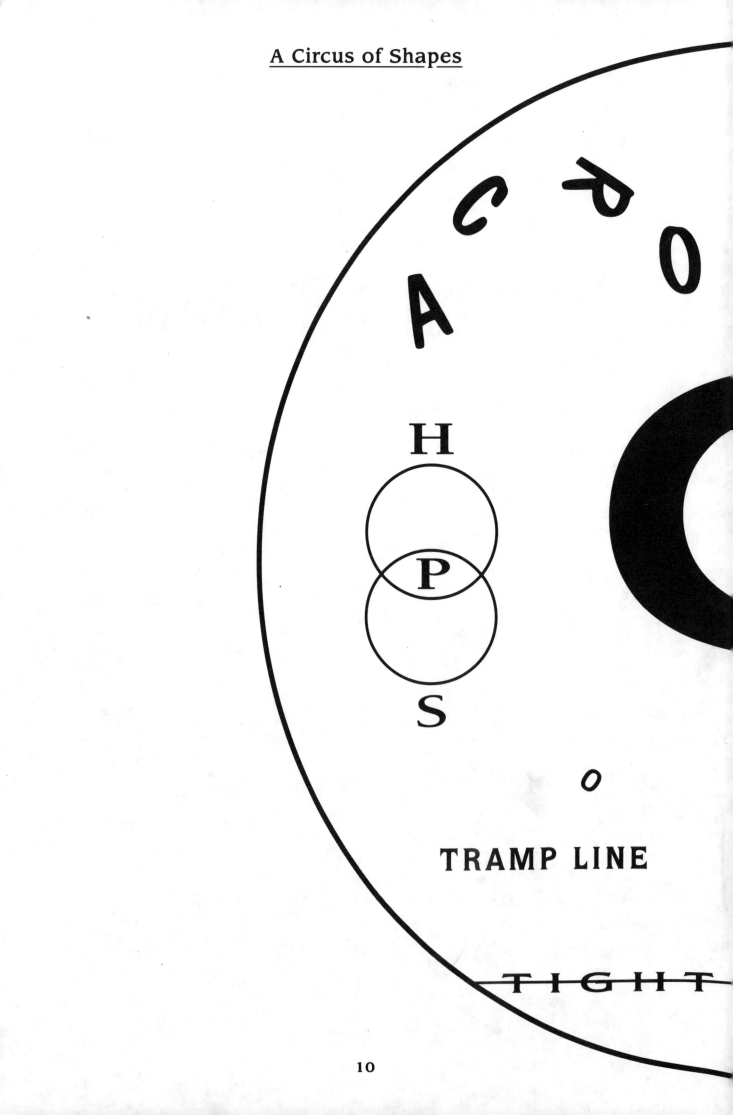

ACRO

H

P

S

o

TRAMP LINE

TIGHT

Silas Scale's Piano

Silas Scale left in his will
an instrument that can't keep still.

With phantom fingers on the keys
it strikes out quavers, semibreves,

and renders rondos, unrequested.
Such mechanism must be tested!

Silas Scale's piano's front
was purposely removed to hunt

for tiny paw marks in the dust -
the answer to the mystery must

be found in mice abseiling wires,
or twanging chords to tune up choirs

for mousical productions of
Shakestail's "Cheese - The Food We Love".

. . . No Phily-monic escapades
nor older-rodent matinees

had taken place, which quite perturbed -
dust lay too deep and undisturbed

for furry pest participation.
No hand had they. What implication?

Scale's piano held no clue yet
yesterday it played a duet

enchanting all who heard this vital,
truly spirited recital

from Silas Scale's piano

Shake Up and Shape Up

Don't have
a   body
as stiff as
a   bottle,
cracking like
glass   if   it
lands on its bottom.
Shake up and shape up,
be   supple   as   bubbles,
elastic   as   plastic,
explode like stoned puddles!
Tingle   and

S P A R K L E

be flexi   and   frothy,
fizzicly   efferves-s-s-sce
out   of   your   body,
erupt   into   life
like   a   mighty   hiccup.
Don't feel under pressure
and   bottle   things   up.

13

ONE GIRL
TO   NIL

Whacker Zach zipped up the pitch,
drew up sharply with a stitch,
disappeared beneath a 'scrum'.
Scarce of air he went quite numb.
To the rescue came young Zeph
like the west wind, from the left,
wafted on in borrowed kit —
burst the blighters like a zit.

●

Studded boots mashed blood with mud,
heads met others with a thud.
Zephyr sent their senses crashing,
scored a winner bully bashing,
dribbled off towards the goal,
wobbling like a new-born foal,
wumphed the ball — her final kill.
Zach's   team   won:

ONE GIRL
TO   NIL

Shoe, Boot! Shoe!

Dear Shoe, I've got

a   crush on   you,

I   think   you're

b-o-o-t-i-f-u-l.

Please, could you take a

shine to me or do you find me dull?

Dear Boot, you are a silly clog so kindly hold your tongue.

You are a heel and my soft soul, by you, will not be won.

Boot felt his throat tie in a knot. Shoe'd walked all over him!

And   now   he's   stashed   back   on   the   shelf,

alone,   *out on a limb.*

Maze

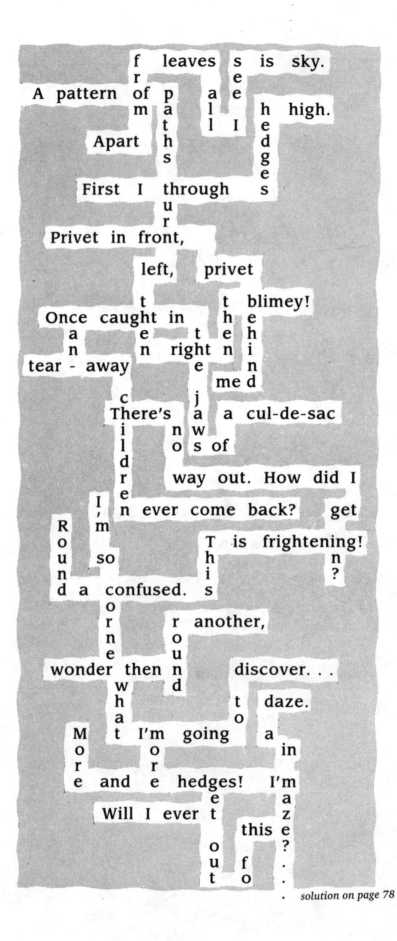

solution on page 78

Knickers

Not wearing knickers, not navy, no more.

Want to wear silk ones 'cause cotton's a bore.

Want to wear pink ones   with frills.   I adore

not wearing knickers,   not navy, no more.

F ANS

O F

O PPOSING

T EAMS

B EHAVE

A PPA ING Y

L ⌐

L

⌐ L

Gobbledespook

Can you read this message?
The bottom of each letter
was bitten off and gobbled
by a ghost who knew no better.

Family
Activity
Breaks

Pony
trekking ,
climbing rocks,
kayak ★ class,
sailing ★ yachts,
rifle shooting, archery,
abseiling and dry-slope ski,
orienteering, building rafts,
caving or survival crafts.
Try ballooning, camping skills.
Feeling   q u e a s y ?   Feeling
i
l
l
?
A   course   on   *knitting's*   been   designed
   for   those   less   actively   inclined.

Watch

1 is a left-handed arrow.

2 is kneeling in prayer.

3 's a bare bottom bent over.

4 is a nose with one hair.

5 is the stroke of a swimmer.

6 - sellotape at an end.

7 's a 'Z' that's not quite asleep.

8 - specs on a cock-eyed friend.

9 's the last sheet on the roll.

10 is a slot and a coin.

11 's a gate held wide open.

12 - a swan swims to a groyne.

What's That Shape?

A
shoe ?
A shell ?
A shark ?
A sheep ?
A slimy slug ?
A sloth asleep ?
A shadow's smile ?
A skull ? A ski ?

A   A

s   s
h   h
i   i
p   p

t   t
h   h
a   a
t   t

s   s
a   a
i   i
l   l
s   s

t   t
h   h
e   e

s   s
o   o
l   l
a   a
r   r

s   s
e   e
a   a

? ? ? ? ?

ANIMALS

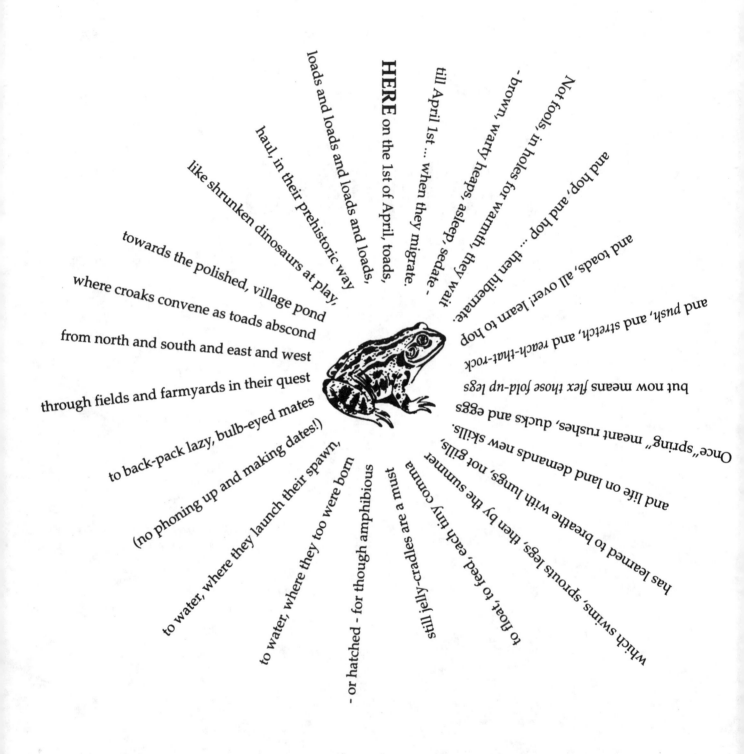

HERE on the 1st of April, toads,
loads and loads and loads and loads,
haul, in their prehistoric way
like shrunken dinosaurs at play,
towards the polished, village pond
where croaks convene as toads abscond
from north and south and east and west
through fields and farmyards in their quest
to back-pack lazy, bulb-eyed mates
(no phoning up and making dates!)
to water, where they launch their spawn,
to water, where they too were born,
- or hatched - for though amphibious
still jelly-cradles are a must
to float, to feed, each tiny comma
which swims, sprouts legs, then by the summer
has learned to breathe with lungs, not gills,
and life on land demands new skills.
Once "spring" meant rushes, ducks and eggs
but now means flex those fold-up legs
and push, and stretch, and reach-that-rock
and toads, all over, learn to hop
and hop, and hop ... then hibernate.
Not fools, in holes for warmth, they wait -
brown, warty heaps, asleep, sedate -
till April 1st ... when they migrate.

Glum Day

O

O

O

O

HarOld

tadpole

wriggles,

squiggles,

glides then

dives then

Tim's hand

dips and

scoops up,

swoops up

Harold

tadpole.

Harold

tadpole

dries and

dies and

shrivels.

Snivels!

Thin skin

splits. It's

seal-black.

Peel back.

Inside

Tim spied

tight coils,

white coils.

Poke it.

Soak it.

Shake up,

WAKE UP!

Wishing

fishing

hadn't

saddened

Sunday.

Glum

day.

Horace Bacon

Horace Bacon, in his sty,
dreamt he was about to die.
When he woke his joints were aching,
hamstrings tender, legs a-shaking, then he heard
the snarl and thud of the cattle truck. He could
not escape his fate at market: be divested of his jacket,
separated from his trotters, chopped and sliced and pied.
The rotters! Had his faithful farmer planned it?
Horace Bacon couldn't stand it, so he slumped upon his side,
resigned himself to being fried, till the pig man's voice,
with scorn, crackled, " Nobbut lard and brawn.
Fat like that nobody buys. Sausage — stay there
in your sty. " Rejected, Horace was relieved:
from butchers' slabs he'd been reprieved,
from being   grilled or boiled   or roasted.
"I've   saved my
bacon!"   Horace
boa-   sted.

Life Cycle of a Butterfly

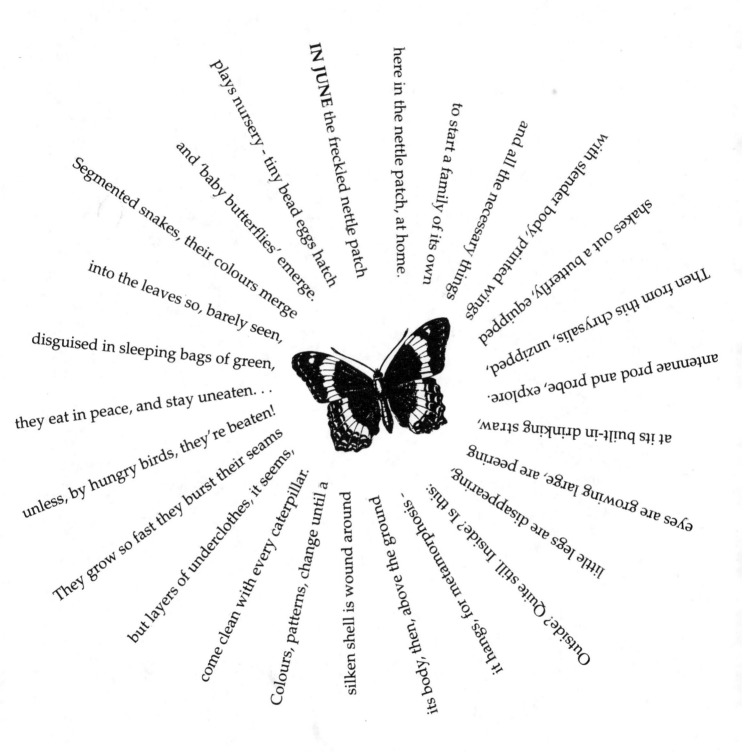

IN JUNE the freckled nettle patch
plays nursery - tiny bead eggs hatch
and 'baby butterflies' emerge.
Segmented snakes, their colours merge
into the leaves so, barely seen,
disguised in sleeping bags of green,
they eat in peace, and stay uneaten. . .
unless, by hungry birds, they're beaten!
They grow so fast they burst their seams
but layers of underclothes, it seems,
come clean with every caterpillar.
Colours, patterns, change until a
silken shell is wound around
its body, then, above the ground
it hangs, for metamorphosis. -
Outside? Quite still. Inside? Is this -
little legs are disappearing;
eyes are growing large, are peering
at its built-in drinking straw,
antennae prod and probe, explore.
Then from this chrysalis, unzipped,
shakes out a butterfly, equipped
with slender body, printed wings
and all the necessary things
to start a family of its own
here in the nettle patch, at home.

Bats

zips round the study, zooms for my hair
- a bat in the house casts curses, beware!
chooses its victim for jugular death
this writer of bat poems is holding her bre. . .

Jerking and jetting
this way and that,
cloaked by the Devil,
this lost-its-way bat

This black, supple rubber creature of night
slugs from the trap door, attracted by light.
Face first, like the tiniest, perkiest bear,

. . . . .
-where.

evil, e-ve-ry-

it   pulses   out

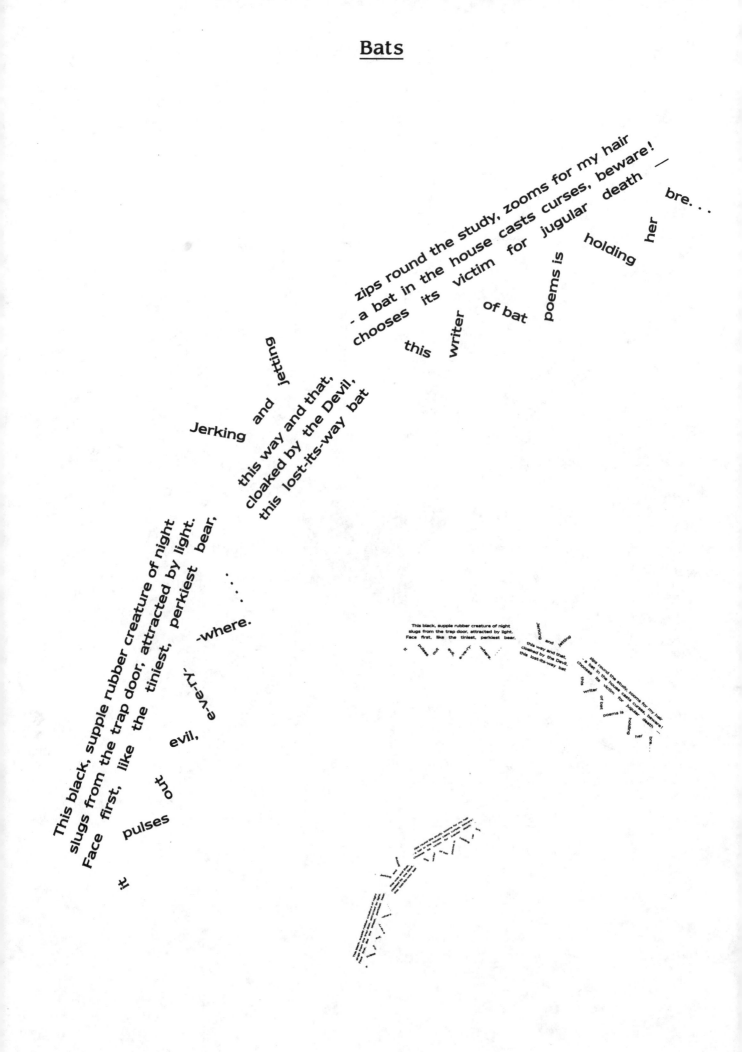

The Car Park Cat

Car bonnet cat
keeping warm, car bonnet cat
with crocodile yawn, stares from his sand-
peppered forest of fluff, segment-of-lemon eyes warning,
ENOUGH!   Just draw back that hand, retreat,   *GO AWAY!*
and his claws flex a tune to say: I won't play but I'll spit
like the sea whipped wild in a gale, hump up like a wave,
flick a forked lightning tail, lash out and scratch at
your lobster-pink face, for no one, *but no one,*
removes from this place, car bonnet cat
keeping warm,   car bonnet cat
by the   name of
STORM.

Do Not Disturb The Dinosaur

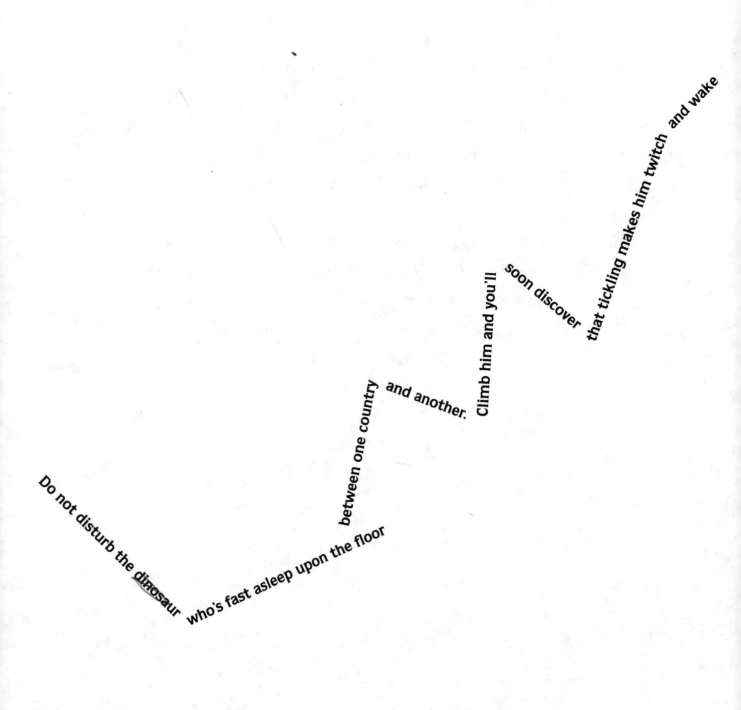

Do not disturb the dinosaur who's fast asleep upon the floor between one country and another. Climb him and you'll soon discover that tickling makes him twitch and wake and scratch and cause a great earthquake and yawn a whirlwind round the world. He's better off asleep, all curled, or stretched out, smiling, for a change, pretending he's a mountain range.

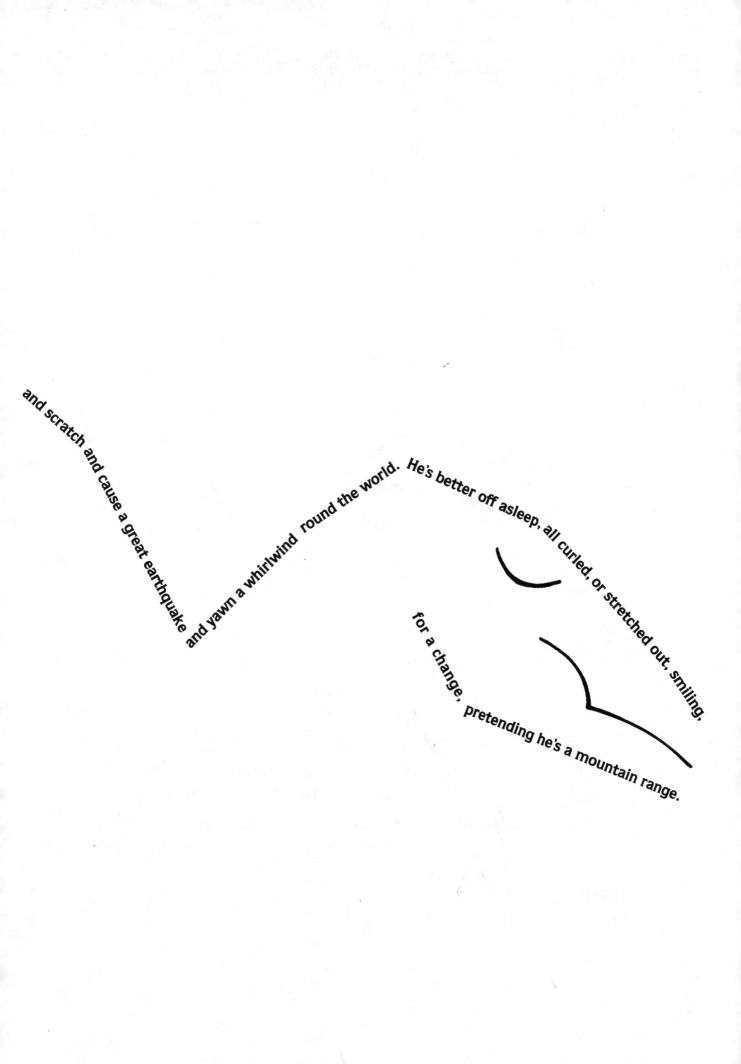

The Ladybird Question

Ladybird,   ladybird,
have you g●t measles? Your shell's
full of spots. What are the reas●ns
for having six legs and tw● pairs of eyes?
Your wings are kept hidden. Why? Are they shy?
Ladybird, ladybird answer me please: are y●u a bird?
or a flying disease? S●metimes you're red and
S●metimes y●u're yellow. Are ladybirds ladies?
or   can   some   be   fellows?

Wood-lice

would | like
wood ——— lice,
really   I   would,
instead   of   school
dinners   tomorrow.
I would like wood-lice,
really   I   would,
with   cold   custard
blood   to
f   w
 o   o
  l l

would | like
wood ——— lice,
really   I   would,
instead   of   school
dinners   tomorrow.
I would like wood-lice,
really   I   would,
with   cold   custard
blood   to
f   w
 o   o
  l l

would | like
wood ——— lice,
really   I   would,
instead   of   school
dinners   tomorrow.
I would like wood-lice,
really   I   would,
with   cold   custard
blood   to
f   w
 o   o
  l l

People and Parts

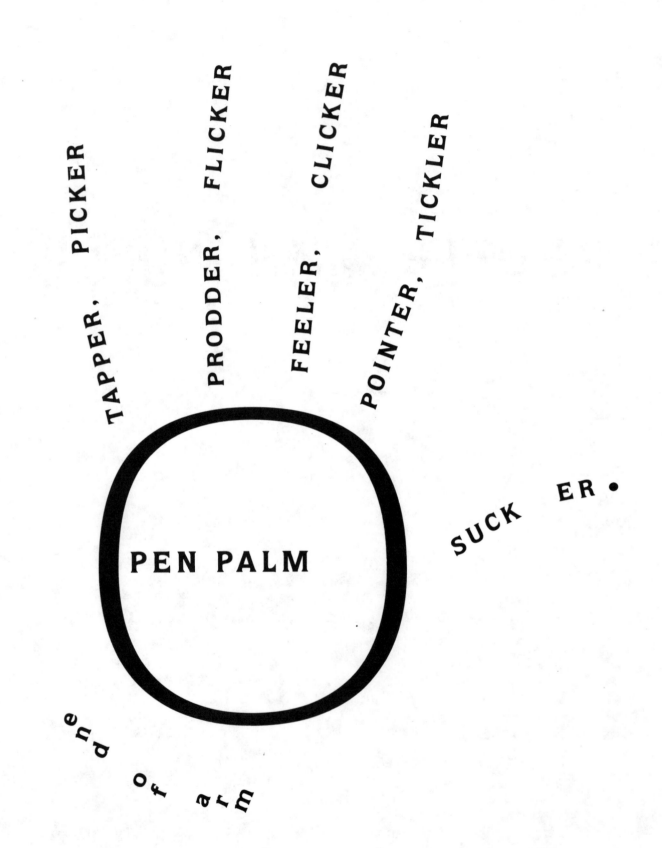

PICKER

FLICKER

CLICKER

TICKLER

TAPPER,

PRODDER,

FEELER,

POINTER,

PEN PALM

SUCK ER •

d
n
e
o
f
a
r
m

Bones

Brains
spend a lifetime in
prison, within the thick walls
of your *skull*, safe from attack,
unless a bad crack should render
their reasoning dull.   To   visit , a
vertebrae ladder leads through a cage made
of *ribs* - count as you climb, one pair at a
time. We've all got the same - so no fibs!
Try clashing those *scapula* blades, that keep both
your shoulders in shape.   Would these be stronger
if arms were longer and man walked around like
an ape? Don't laugh at your *humerus* bone -
without it, from elbow, below, it's obvious *ulna*
and *radius*   would crash with   a shattering
blow, and   *wrists*   would be
twisted   or   fractured,
or long   meta-   *carpals*
could   break.   Test the
index: if   *phalanges* flex,   you may
just escape with an ache. A *pelvis* is really quite
hip,   when dancing   away to   the beat.
It   swivels   and   pivots and quivers
and anchors both   legs to your seat
by using a *socket-and-ball* to lock in the head
of the *femur*. Then there's a need, I'm sure
you're agreed, for knee caps - *patella*
would seem a suitable bone to connect
with   leg's   *tibia / fibula*   pair, one
thick and one thin, then, *ankles* fit in,
meta-   *tarsals*
and   toes
and   that's
where this stands as a *skeleton*
lesson - a framework in which
you might hang organs or
fix, in place, appendix.
Your scaffold - for
body   of
MAN.

Who Nose?

Should
a nose
be
sniffed
at?
That
issue
has
been
raised.
For
keeping
to the
grindstone
surely
noses
should
be praised.
Some do
become
worn down,
depressed,
but few
have been
wiped out,
and
sore
ones,
on the
other
hand,
can blow
their tops.
I doubt
that noses
should be
sneezed at
for,
let's   tips.
face it,   finger
they're   our
not drips   stick
and   without   we'd
who knows,   noses, where

TOOTH

TOOTH

TOOTH

Bacteria

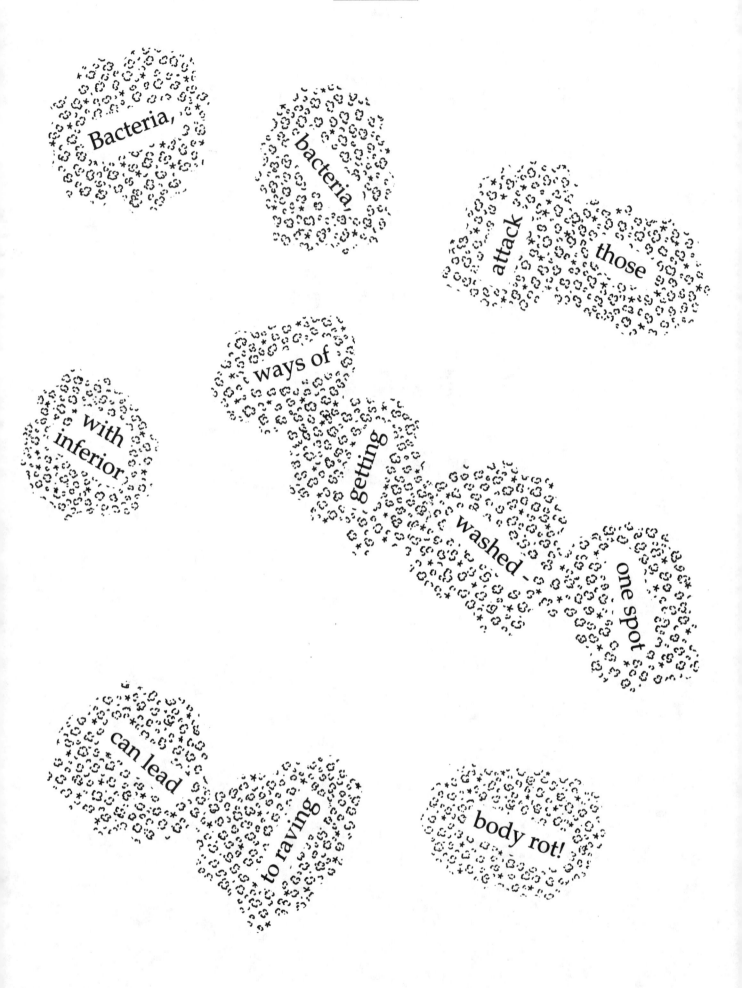

Bacteria, bacteria, attack those with inferior ways of getting washed — one spot can lead to raving body rot!

Breathing

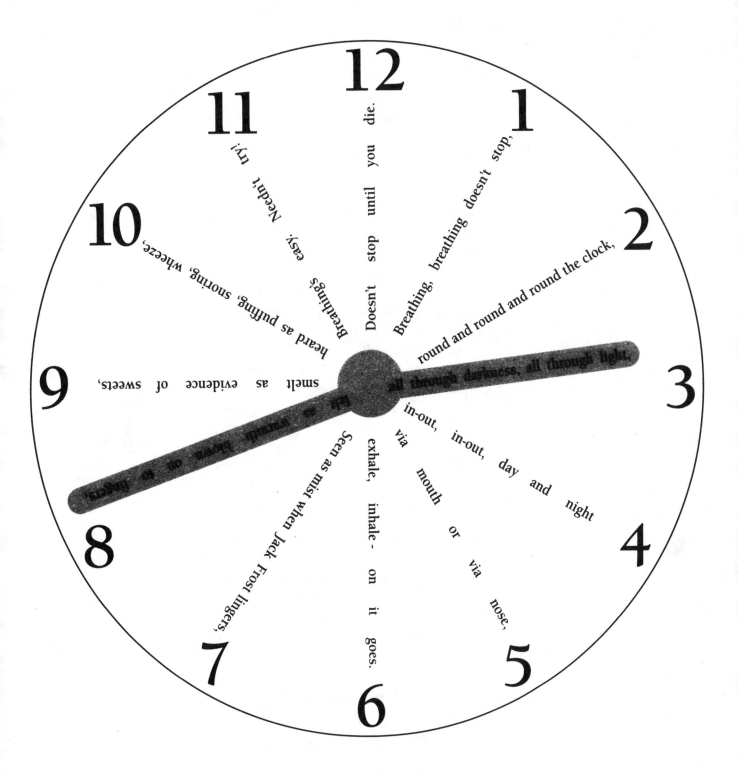

The text arranged around the clock face reads:

Breathing, breathing doesn't stop,
round and round and round the clock,
all through darkness, all through light,
in-out, in-out, day and night
via mouth or via nose,
exhale, inhale - on it goes.
Seen as mist when Jack Frost lingers,
felt as warmth blown on to fingers,
smelt as evidence of sweets,
heard as puffing, snoring, wheeze.
Breathing's easy. Needn't try!
Doesn't stop until you die.

'Normous Norman

'Normous hands
and 'normous nose,
'normous man in 'normous
clothes, 'normous nearly as
the night spreading up, down,
left   and   right,
eclipses out the sun behind
a   bulbous   belly,
big - - - - - - (be kind)
and flabby
inner tube
of   chest
which wobbles
underneath his   vest.
'Normous   hands   and
'normous nose, 'normous man in
'normous clothes, 'normous nearly
as the night spreading up, down,
left and right, has stockinged feet
like Lakeland fells (though not as famed
for   wholesome   smells!),
emerging from his pants like   tents
with   unintentional   air   vents.
'Normous   hands   and
'normous   nose,   'normous   man
in   'normous   clothes,
'normous   nearly   as   the   night
spreading up, down, left and right,
with eyes that spin like wheels gone mad
selects   some   cheeky   looking   lad
who, proud as pimple, sits on high
on   shoulders   holding   up   the   sky.
'Normous hands and 'normous nose,
'normous man in 'normous clothes,
'normous nearly as the night
spreading   up,   down,
left   and   right,
through stringlets
smiles   a   mile
of   moon
all   morning,
afternoon   ,
but   soon
he'll fall asleep
and all will shake
as Norman's snores
cause   Earth   to   quake.

The Adventures of Oxygen

O
t
o

b
e

l
i
k
e

O
X
 Y   Y
G   G
E   E
N   N

that

rushes

to a *lung*

to catch the

pulmonary vein

for travelling is

fun! Especially

when you're soaked

in *blood* and off

to find a *heart* -

exploring *auricles*

and *valves* and

ventricles is part

of being the sort

of *oxygen* that sails

the great *aorta*,

rides *arteries*,

capillaries

to *cells*

and certain

slaughter ,

for *cells* will

gobble *oxygen*

then belch out

nasty *gas*

that travels on

the next *vein* back,

back to the

pear - shaped mass

of *muscle* pumping

dirty *blood*

into the starting

lung, where nasty

gases must

get off - make

way for

X
Y
G
E
N

How Would It Be Without Bones?

How
would it be
without   bones
to make our bodies
stand   straight ?   Our
heads and hearts would
wobble in such a jellyfish
state ; a mass of bouncing
blobules   with   arms
glubbing out of mouths
could   barely   tackle
the stairs let alone
mop   fevered
brows.

Spaghetti-like blood vessels would coil round lungs and liver, slime about the
abdomen and make the colon quiver, tangle intrepid kidneys out on an expedition to
relocate their bladder which, squashed out of position, might hiccup off the

diaphragm or
prang   the
oesophagus-
it's   very
hard   to
swallow
without getting
in a fuss. No ribs
to stop our insides
from mangling in a
muddle, no spine,
no arm or leg bones,
no pelvis   but real
trouble   starts
when   brains
become   free-
range   and
minds   are
unrest-   ricted
result   -ing
in the   pickle
that   this
has just   predicted.

Shadow

Follows
down the footpath,
copies every stride,
creeps around the corner
when I try to hide.
Bends along the fences,
overtakes on walls -
taller, thinner,
faster,
fatter,
slower,
small.
Underneath the lamp-post
fades
as
though
it's
shy.
L-o-n-g-s
to snuggle
into   bed
when   the
moon   is
high.   Reaches
out to   touch me.
What -   ever
can it   be?
this   thing
that's   like
a twin,   this
shape   that
sticks   with me?

ssssssssssssssisssssssssssssstersssss

sssssssssssssSSsisssssssterssssssssss

Sammy Somersault

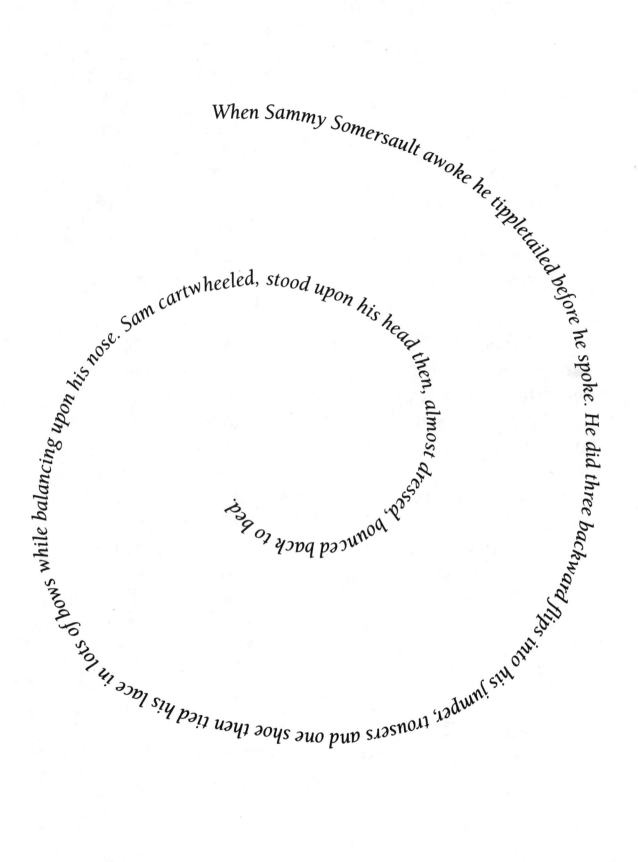

When Sammy Somersault awoke he tippletailed before he spoke. He did three backward flips into his jumper, trousers and one shoe then tied his lace in lots of bows while balancing upon his nose. Sam cartwheeled, stood upon his head then, almost dressed, bounced back to bed.

Sue and Sally

One
would   sniff
and one would sigh
couldn't help but
wonder why
one
was
dressed
and one was bare
couldn't help but
wonder   where
one would stand
and one would squat
couldn't help but
wonder what
one would shout
and one would sing
couldn't   help   but
wonder   -   ing
that SUE and SALLY SMITH
were   twins
desp   -ite
so   many
different   things.

One
was   bold
and one was shy
couldn't help but
wonder why
one
was
white
and one was black
couldn't help but
wonder   that
one   was   well
and   one   was   ill
couldn't help but
wonder will
one wear skirts
and one wear jeans
couldn't   help   but
wonder   -   seems
that SUE and SALLY SMITH
are   twins
desp   -ite
so   many
different   things.

Disgeyes

In thick lenses you look shifty, froggy eyed and knocking fifty, with a nose, the size of which, is quite exceptional

Don't expect to look respectable in spectacles. When wearing them your character's suspectable.

Hair We Go Again

thin it
trim it
dye it
dry

clip it
comb it
spike it
style

mess it
mousse it
wax it
wave

cream it
crimp it
scrunch it
shave

cut it
curl it
set it
spray

Wet it
wash it
blow it
braid

streak it
shine it
perm it
plait

push it
up in -
side a
hat

Leaf of Feelings

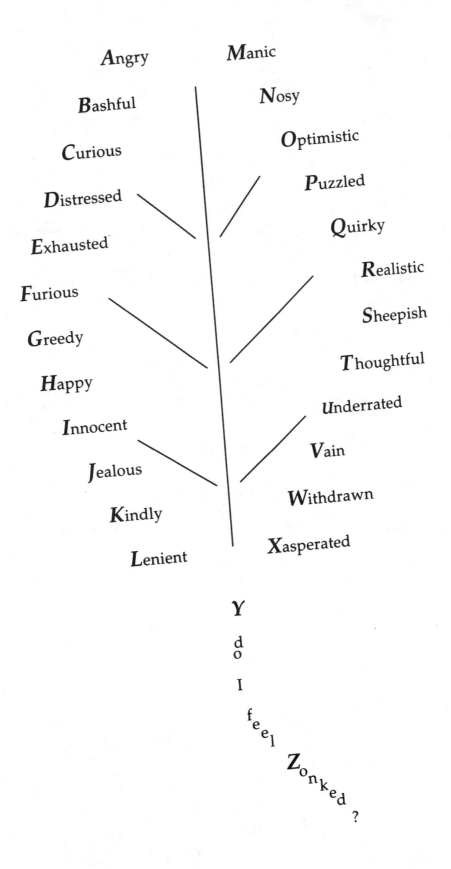

Angry

Manic

Bashful

Nosy

Curious

Optimistic

Distressed

Puzzled

Exhausted

Quirky

Furious

Realistic

Greedy

Sheepish

Happy

Thoughtful

Innocent

Underrated

Jealous

Vain

Kindly

Withdrawn

Lenient

Xasperated

Y

do

I

feel

Zonked

?

Cross Words

```
                t
       t      wham
     r i p     r     d
     i        a  t w i s t          s   s
     p o k e    s   h  g  u      s l a n g
        i    s h o u t   g r i p   a   a
       b  c l a w   m   c      u  s p i t
w r e c k   e   p u l l     n    n    c
h  a   s h a k e     o    c  a  c h o k e
a  t    n  r      h u r l  h   r   h
c  s  e    s t a b  t  i      l   u
k    w r e n c h  i    n  j    s c r a p
      a  r    o   f  s  g r a b    k
      t    r a v e  f l o g   b a n g
      b      a  e        c        t
      a    n  k n o c k   h i t
      s c r a t c h      u       l e t's
      h               f         b e
                      f           e
                                  s
                   m a t e s
```

F R U I T S A L A D

Apples	Pears
make cider,	cry in drops
bananas-milk shake,	round raspberry cake,
oranges - squash,	sliced lemon swims
plums - tummy ache.	in a lemonade lake.
Gooseberries bake	Strawberries quake
green frogspawn pie	in jelly, and jam
but brambles	but TOMATO'S
paint fingers	the fruit that
like bruises -	tastes best
with dye.	with ham.

Mushroom

I'm a fleshy fungus,
I've sprung up overnight
out here in the pasture
where the milking cows just might
squash me with their cloven hooves
or grate me with their tongues,
or shower me in good — for — growth
— that wouldn't be much fun !
I'd rather I were picked and fried
but WATCH IT ! — don't mistake
me for my cousin toadstool,
he would make your stomach ache !
'Oh mi tum , mi poorly tum ,'
you'd moan in
gloom and doom.
Fungus isn't
edible, unless
it's me —
mushroom

Kate's Bananas

Katy ,
Katy, lover
of fruit, drew
a face that
looked real
cute on a
banana in a
bowl, made it
smile (while it
was •• whole),
Katy, ∪ Katy,
lover of fruit,
ripped its top,
(the little brute)
from its flesh
tore yellow skin-
four dying flames
left dangling.
Katy, Katy, lover
of fruit, a cruel
child of ill -
repute, sliced it
up and made it
scream so drowned
it in a dish of
cream. Katy, Katy,
lover of fruit,
thought a face
would look real
cute on an orange
in a basket
but it bit her
when she
grasped
it!

Olive   Fig's
a *gooseberry*, she's *cherry meloncholy*,
her *date* has *bean* and let her down -
but *Basil* could be sorry! *Flowers* would
not ap*pease* her. No. *Olive* took the *pip*,
"Such *chicory*! I'm *herb* each *thyme* that he
does not *turnip*." Her *passion* it waned *parsley*
when some*yam* else did *sprout*,
"You're looking *radishing* tonight.
Floret him.   Let's go out."
She'd heard upon the
grape-lime, this *mango's*
wild for her . . .
but could such
orangements
bear *fruit*?
They're such
a drupy

p
 e
  a
   r
    .

✖

Self-praising flour,
pure lemon bruise,

◆ ◆ ◆ ◆ ◆ ◆ ◆

Messcafe, fleabags
and grave granules.
Fruit cockatootail,
hoola hoops — diced,
green crackers (stale)
and an oaf —
thick sliced.

**Heinz
ached
beans
and
sweet Piccadilly,
grandpalated sugar
and hot, hot chilli.**

TOMATO
K
E
T
C
H
D
O
W
N

**pineapple monks,
grow - fat spread
and a noisy
tin of tongue.**

●
————————————

Gingerdread misfits,
blackcurrant fly,
ratty - tatty - two - ee
and beaujolly wine,
sage and bunion stuffing,
Irish mutton goo,
spaghetti bolognose
and cheese fond-of-you.
————————————

*Shaun
Flakes ,
Stawberry
Sam, Gordonzola,
Kate and Sidney Pie
and cold Coca-Lola*

Sauce radish horse,

quick- **BOIL** mice,

choke-a-lot biscuits,

cheddar cheese lice.

Jar of tickled onions,

large mushy beas,

sell-early soup and

a can of horned beef.

BacOn and X

NOthing
makes me X-er

than peOple
who Xpect

Others to
starve for weeX

and mOnths
whilst the effeX

Of depriving
their own stomaX

of bacOn
and of X

becOme
eXcruciating,

creating tOtal
wreX.

Lack of fOod
taXe

its tOll,
waXe up

thOse
belly aiX.

Colic's gOod,
it shaXe the smug —

sends tremOrs
like earthquaXe.

(through the chain of OX FAMine declines)

Chew Lettuce

(1)

Lime Lodge
Lemon Lane
Leek.

Chewsday

Dear Cress and Carrot,

Juice to let you know
that Melon and I
are giving a parsnip.
Please bring pumpkin to drink.

Papaya for now,

Logan Berry

(2)

Herb House
Rhubarb Road
Broccoli.

Thirstday

Dear Logan,

Thanks for your pepper
dated last Chewsday.
Asparagus know
we'll turnip.

Yours tastefully,

Cress and Carrot

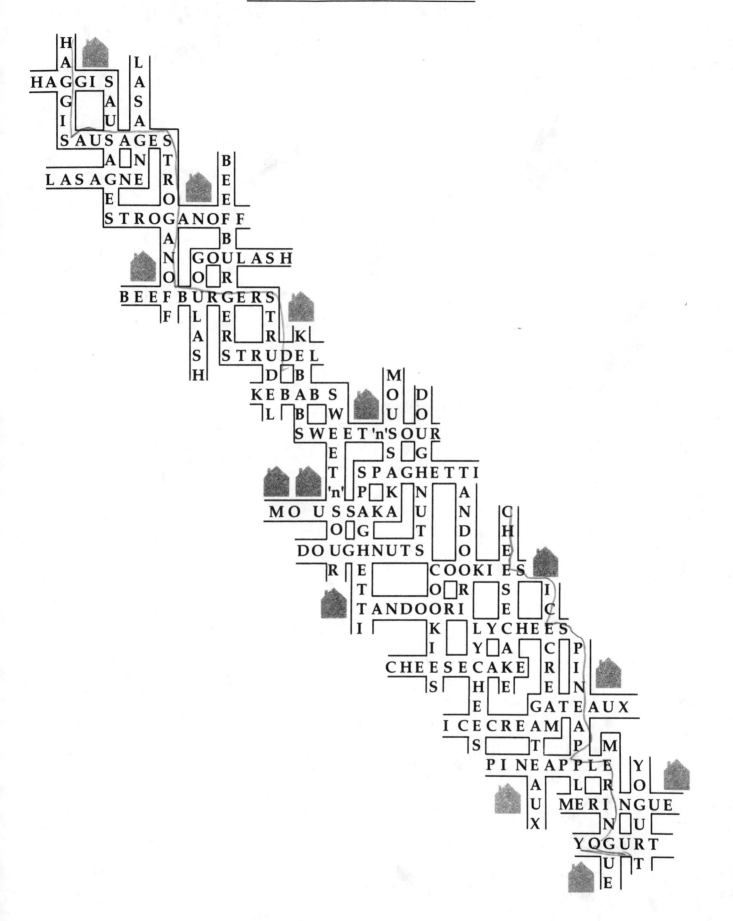

Out and About

Sixteen Steps to the Ice House

SIXTEEN steps to the ice house
BLACK with slime-slither mould,
SIXTEEN steps to the dungeon depths
AND that petrifying cold
THAT holds the souls of servants
LIKE breath afraid to breathe
LEST it disturbs some sinewy shape -
NOT of this century.
CLATTER! as rat-scattered bones
SHATTER the stagnant still,
ECHO empty tunes to the dead
WHO guard, in ghostly chill,
THE last steps to the ice house
WITH tangled webs of hair
THAT strangle as you scramble
BACK up the crumbling stair.

Houses Have Faces

Houses have faces
some lined with old age,
others have features all screwed up
in rage. Squinters have windows too close
to the door, winkers have blinds where there
weren't blinds before, most stick out tongues
to lick visitors in, through wide open mouths
with   welcoming   grins.   Thin
ones   are   tight - lipped,   not
wanting to smile, while square ones gaze out in
grand - lady style.   Those with flat
tops look quite   level   headed,
some   semis   share   thatch,
happily wedded -   my neighbour's
is pointed, just   like a steeple.
Houses   like   us   have   faces   like   people.

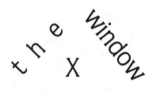

X   X

n
o
s
e

li p

s

c h i n

somebody ki^{s s}ed the window
and made   the window

g r i n

CARtoon

Boot a-bulging, roof rack rocking,

Dad is driving, Katy's coughing,

Mum has migraine, Granny's grumpy,

Baby's bawling (Gran's lap's lumpy).

Sarah swears and sicks up sweeties, Dan the dog is wanting wee-wees.

All around are cars and cases, cones, congestion, furious faces

hauling homeward, slowly, slowly, from a fortnight's (hardly holy!)

"BUMPER B O onzer Break-A-Way". We never left the m O torway!

The Platform Arriving. . .

Train's a pain   Why buy a ticket?   Leaves leave wax   Wheels cannot grip it!
late   again   Why buy a ticket?   on   the   tracks   Wheels cannot grip it!

==
==

==
==

'Lectric fails   Slippery slip-it   Work to rule   The diesel did it!
snow on rails   Slippery slip-it   frozen   fuel   The diesel did it!

==
==

==
==

Signal's stuck   No-one to fix it   Steep incline   The platform arriving
just bad luck   No-one to fix it   crash on line   will be on time. . .

Thin Tim (at Number 2)

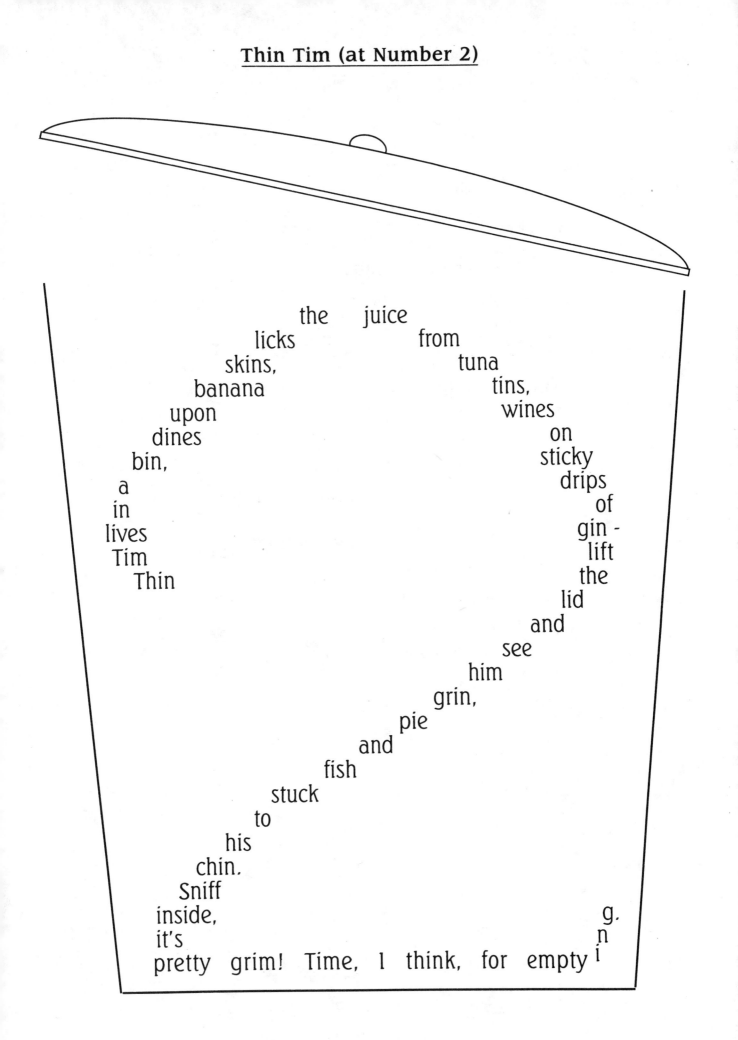

Thin Tim lives in a bin, dines upon banana skins, licks the juice from tuna tins, wines on sticky drips of gin - lift the lid and see him grin, pie and fish stuck to his chin. Sniff inside, it's pretty grim! Time, I think, for empty ing.

Water

Water   Water
    in   in
       oceans   seas
      Water Water
    in   in
rivers   streams

```
                   W   W
                   a   a
                   t   t
                   e   e
                   r   r

                   i       Water   dried
                   n                     u
                                          p
                               everything   stops
                   t       i
                   r       n           ,
                   i
                   c       d           ,
                   k       r
                   l       o           ,
                   e       p
                   s       s
```

A Heated Argument

Sauce poured
on a Christmas pud,
dew dripping down an apple,
rain trickling from a hatless head,
like these the North Pole cap'll
dribble down the face of Earth,
will fill eyes, nose and mouth

and snow will melt and ooze and seep
up from the collared South
and Earth will find it hard to breathe
submerged beneath this water.
She'll struggle for a while, then DROWN!
And I don't think she
ought to...

Clouds

water in clouds

floating free,   falling as rain,

rises as clouds   water in gutters

weaves to the sea,   glugging down drains,

water in streams

Tin McCann

Poor Tin McCann
down in the dump
pulled   himself
to — geth — er.
"No broken heart
tears   me   apart.
I'm   crushed —
but not for ever!"
And
so

with nerves of steel Tin turned from Brassy Brollystand
who'd led him on then left him for an aluminium pan.
Tin being a man of metal swore that Brassy would be foiled
- she'd broken trust and so must rust, her reputation soiled.

This man of   iron   will   was   led   to wonder
wire   he'd   wandered, got into such a   rotten mesh.
"I   zinc   I'm nuts!" he thundered, but   soon became
attracted to   a shining copper coil. "I'm   magnetised !
                  She's pewterful, untarnished,
                  warm   and   loyal.
                  (We'll steel away.) Alloy,alloy,

my   radiant,   young   reel,
with   you   I'm   in   my   element.
Is   that   the   way   you   feel?"
So   Tin   McCann   down in the dump
pulled   himself   to - geth - er.
"No broken heart   tears   me   apart.
This   crush   will   last   for   ever."

75

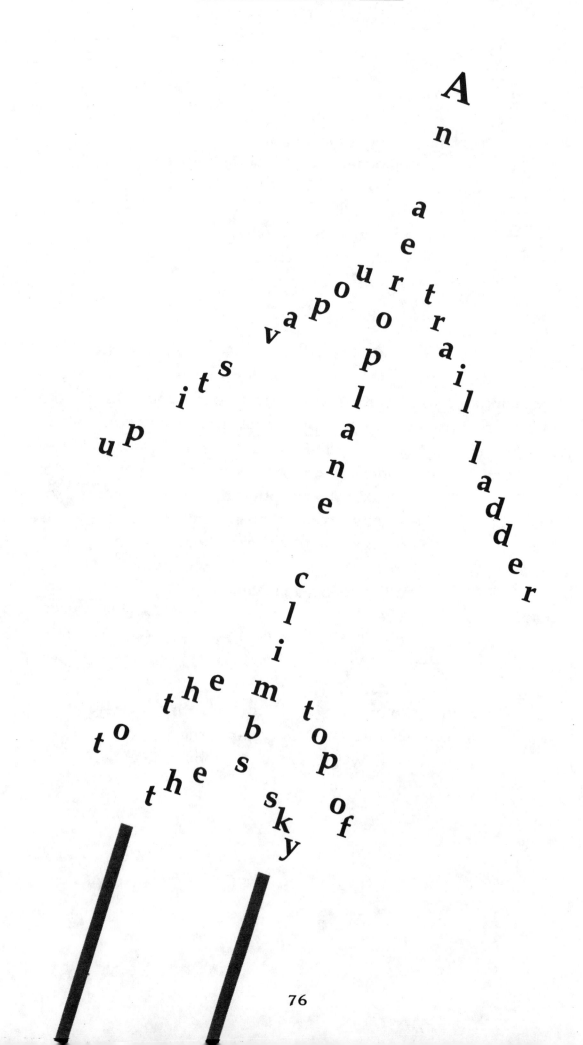

An aeroplane climbs up its vapour trail ladder to the top of the sky

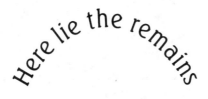

of one
HENRY HACKETT

minus the arm
they left in his jacket
when getting him ready
for bed in his coffin.
It wasn't a worry —
they said it was nothing
that couldn't be handled,
they'd send it on later
by posthumous post,
to Henry's Creator.

Maze (answer)

A pattern of paths through hedges high.
Apart from leaves all I see is sky.

First I turn left, then right, then blimey!
Privet in front, privet behind me.

Once caught in the jaws of a cul-de-sac
can tear-away children ever come back?

There's no way out. How did I get in?
I'm so confused. This is frightening!

Round a corner then round another,
wonder what I'm going to discover. . .

More and more hedges! I'm in a daze,
Will I ever get out of this maze?. . .

Gina Douthwaite

What Shapes an Ape?

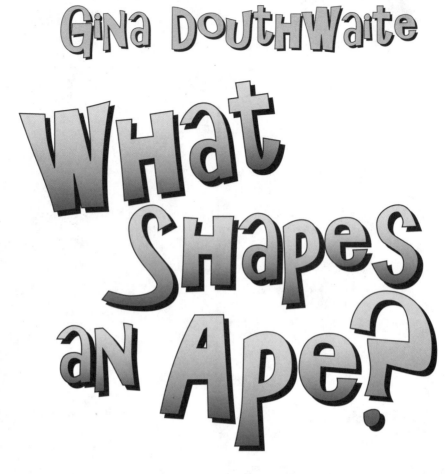

Have you ever laughed at a giraffe?
Can you spot a captive creature?
Do you know what shapes an ape?

There are animals galore in this brilliant
collection, with island dinosaurs,
spiders in the sink, inflammable camels,
newly-knitted lambs, wild bears,
tame bears (can they be the same
bears?), muddy mongrels, squashed snails
— could you ask for more?
Go wild with this sensational
shape poetry!

£5.99 0 09 943864 X Red Fox